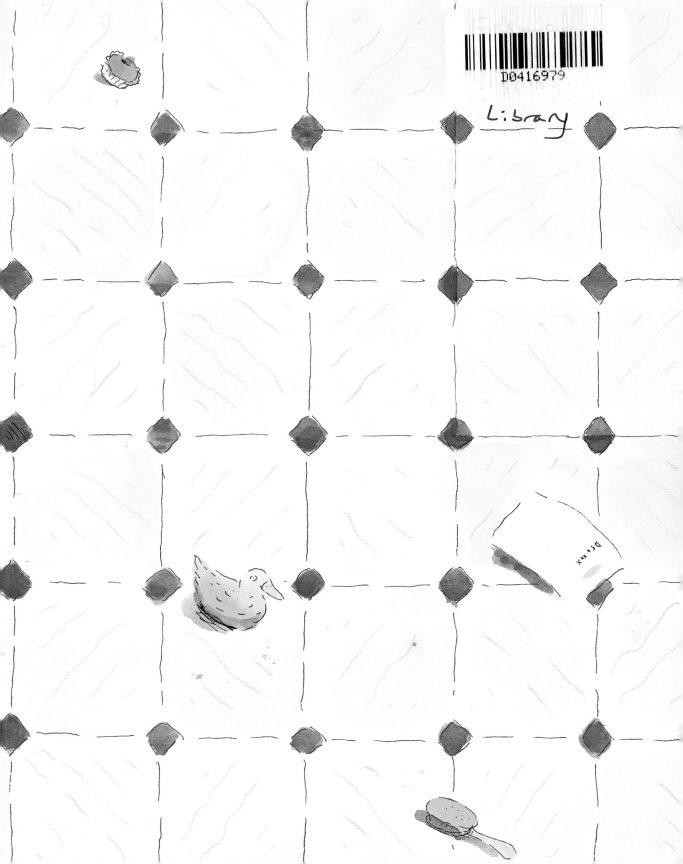

D0416979

For Chlöe and Theo

Fun-to-Read Picture Books have been
grouped into three approximate readability
levels by Bernice and Cliff Moon. Yellow
books are suitable for beginners; red books
for readers acquiring first fluency; blue
books for more advanced readers.

This book has been assessed as Stage 7
according to *Individualised Reading*, by
Bernice and Cliff Moon, published by
The Centre for the Teaching of Reading,
University of Reading
School of Education.

First published 1986 by
Walker Books Ltd
184-192 Drummond Street
London NW1 3HP

First printed 1986
Printed and bound by
L.E.G.O., Vicenza, Italy

British Library Cataloguing in Publication Data
Voake, Charlotte
Tom's cat. — (Fun-to-read picture books)
I. Title   II. Series
823'.914[J]   PZ7

ISBN 0-7445-0527-5

TOM'S CAT

WRITTEN AND ILLUSTRATED BY
Charlotte Voake

WALKER BOOKS
LONDON

Here is Tom

looking for his cat.

CLICK CLICK CLICK

Is that Tom's cat
walking across the floor?

No. It's Grandma knitting socks again.

click click click

TAP TAP TAP

Is that Tom's cat?

Is he dancing on the table?

No.

Tom's mother is typing

a letter to her friend.

tap tap tap

SPLASH SPLASH SPLASH

Is that Tom's cat?

No. Cats hate water.

So does Tom's brother.
But here he is,
trying to wash his hair.

CLATTER

CLATTER

CLATTER

What's that?

Is that Tom's cat

bringing everyone

a cup of tea?

No.

That's Tom's dad...

making pancakes.

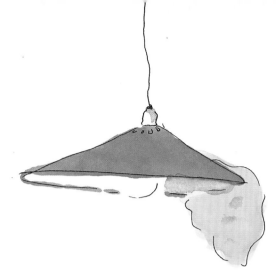

And what's this loud noise?

VROOM

VROOM

VROOM

It sounds a bit like

Tom's cat on a...

MOTORBIKE!

But no.

It's Tom's sister

quickly cleaning the carpet

before anyone sees

she's dropped the cake

on the floor.

So where is Tom's cat?